*By* Dee Lillegard

*Illustrated by* Jillian Lund

Dutton Children's Books

# Tortoise Brings the Mail

CIP Data is available.

Published in the United States 1997 by Dutton Children's Books,
a division of Penguin Books USA Inc.
375 Hudson Street, New York, New York 10014

Designed by Semadar Megged

Printed in Hong Kong    First Edition
ISBN 0-525-45156-0
2 4 6 8 10 9 7 5 3 1

 ay out in the countryside, there lived a tortoise whose job was to carry the mail.

Tortoise loved his job. He put all the mail in all the right boxes, and he was nice and friendly. But everybody thought he was too slow.

One day Crow said, "I can do better than Tortoise. I can fly in a straight line. I can go fast."

Everybody else said, "Let's let Crow bring our mail."

Tortoise had to agree. "Delivering the mail is very important. Let the very best one do it."

So Crow got the job that Tortoise loved.

Poor Tortoise. I may as well just lie in the sun and snooze, he said to himself. But after a while...

A letter came floating down out of the air and landed on Tortoise's nose.

"My goodness," he said. "I'd better help Crow deliver this letter."

Then another letter drifted down, and another, for Crow was dropping the mail as he flew.

Letters landed on treetops and rooftops, and in places nobody could reach. There was a big fuss all over the countryside.

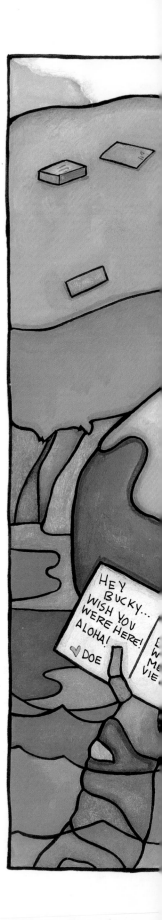

"Nobody appreciates me," said Crow. "I quit."
And he flew away home with his feathers ruffled.
    Tortoise was so happy to have his old job back.
He hummed and smiled to himself. Until...

Rabbit said, "I can do better than Tortoise and Crow. I can run fast. And I will put the mail in the mailboxes."

Everybody else said, "Let's let Rabbit bring our mail."

Tortoise had to agree. "Delivering the mail is very important. Let the very best one do it."

So Rabbit got the job that Tortoise loved.

Poor Tortoise. He lay in the sun and snoozed until...loud shouts woke him.

"This isn't my letter!" "This isn't my package!"

It seems that Rabbit had gone racing through bushes and hopping over logs. She had put everything in the mailboxes. But...

Rabbit ran so fast, she did not have time to read names. She put all the letters and packages in the wrong mailboxes.

"My goodness," said Tortoise, "I'd better help Rabbit learn who's who."

There was a big fuss all over the countryside. Rabbit stopped in her tracks.

"Nobody appreciates me," she said. "I quit." And she dragged herself home, all tuckered out.

Tortoise went all over the countryside, taking the mail from the wrong boxes and putting it in the right ones. It took him half the evening.

But Tortoise was so happy to have his old job back. He hummed and smiled to himself. Until…

Fox said, "I can do better than Tortoise and Crow and Rabbit. I'm fast and I'm smart. And I never make mistakes."

Everybody else said, "Let's let Fox bring our mail."

Again, Tortoise had to agree. "Delivering the mail is very important. Let the very best one do it."

So Fox got the job that Tortoise loved.

Fox was not very friendly. But he whizzed through the bushes. He leaped over logs. He read each name and put every piece of mail into the right box.

Well, *almost* every piece of mail...

You see, Fox sniffed everything first. And when he smelled a package he liked, he kept it for himself. Nobody fussed about this. They had no idea what Fox was up to. They thought he was doing a great job.

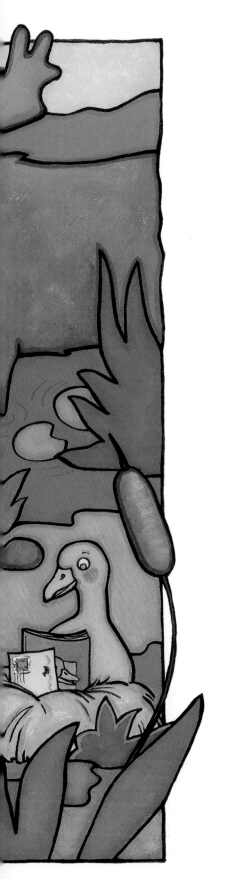

Poor Tortoise. He was getting very tired of lying in the sun. "I think I will take a walk," he said one Sunday morning.

Tortoise walked along his old mail route until he came to Fox's house.

"Fox should be home today," said Tortoise. "I will stop and congratulate him on the great job he is doing."

Tortoise knocked on Fox's door. But there was no answer. Tortoise knocked again and then stepped inside. To his surprise, Tortoise saw all the packages that Fox had kept for himself.

"My goodness," said Tortoise. "Fox has gotten behind in his work. I will help him deliver these packages, even though it's Sunday."

So Tortoise took the packages and began to deliver them. It took him all day and half the evening.

"But why didn't Fox bring us our packages?" everybody asked Tortoise when they saw him.

"Delivering the mail is a big job," said Tortoise.

He was happy to be helping Fox. And he was happy to be doing his old job.

When Fox came home and saw that all his treasures were gone, he was furious!

"Everything is gone!" Fox shouted.

Just then, Tortoise stopped by on his way back.

"Don't worry, Fox," he said. "I delivered the packages for you."

Fox took a deep breath and smiled a toothy smile. "Thank you, my friend," he said.

"You're very welcome," said Tortoise. "I want to congratulate you on the great job you're doing."

"How very nice of you," said Fox.

Clever Tortoise, Fox thought. He has outfoxed me. He knows I meant to keep those packages. But he is much too clever to say so. That night Fox packed his bags and left the forest forever.

The next day, Tortoise was surprised to learn that Fox was gone.

He was even more surprised when, all over the countryside, everybody else said, "From now on, Tortoise, we want you to bring our mail. Now we know, you are the very best one."

Tortoise beamed. "My goodness," he said. "I'd better get busy."

Then off he went to deliver the mail. He hummed and smiled to himself—for Tortoise loved his job!